BATTER
SPLATTER

With love to the real Caitlynne
—C.D.

To Christian, Claire and Marie-Pierre,
with love
—G.K.

Kane Press
An imprint of Astra Books for Young Readers,
a division of Astra Publishing House
kanepress.com
Printed in the United States

Library of Congress Cataloging-in-Publication Data

Names: Daly, Catherine R., author. | Kote, Genevieve, illustrator.
Title: Batter splatter / by Catherine R. Daly ;
illustrated by Genevieve Kote.
Description: First edition. | New York : Kane Press, an imprint of Astra
Books for Young Readers, 2024. | Series: Dollars to doughnuts |
Audience: Ages 6-9. | Audience: Grades 2-3. | Summary: The members of
Julian and Lucy's cooking club plan a bake sale fundraiser to repair a
school banner after a kitchen disaster destroys it, but they need to
understand how to stick to a budget in order to be successful.
Identifiers: LCCN 2023026163 | ISBN 9781662670565 (hardcover) |
ISBN 9781662670237 (trade paperback) | ISBN 9781662670244 (ebk)
Subjects: CYAC: Budget—Fiction. | Cooking—Fiction. | Schools—Fiction. |
LCGFT: Novels.
Classification: LCC PZ7.D175 Bat 2024 | DDC [Fic]—dc23
LC record available at https://lccn.loc.gov/2023026163

2 4 6 8 10 9 7 5 3 1

BATTER
SPLATTER

by Catherine R. Daly
illustrated by Genevieve Kote

KANEPRESS
AN IMPRINT OF ASTRA BOOKS FOR YOUNG READERS
New York

CHAPTER ONE

BRRRRRIIIIINNNNGGG!

Julian nearly jumped out of his skin
when the end-of-the-school-day bell rang.
But unlike most days, he wasn't excited
for the afternoon to begin. Today was
Thursday, and that meant cooking club.
He took his time packing up his backpack.

Lucy wasn't moving any faster. She
put her pencils away in their case super
carefully. When the two friends were
finally ready, they headed into the hallway.

"What do you think we're going to make in cooking club today?" Lucy asked.

Julian snorted. "Peanut butter and jelly sandwiches? Or maybe fruit salad?"

"Yeah, right." Lucy shook her head. "Those would both need a knife."

Julian and Lucy had joined their school's cooking club with high hopes. They imagined making fancy homemade pizzas and seven-layer cakes. But they soon found out that the club adviser, Ms. Clark, wouldn't let them use anything sharp or that needed to be plugged in. As a result, cooking class wasn't exactly a lot of fun.

The hallway was busy, and a little kid in

the third grade bumped right into Julian.
"Sorry!" he shouted. "I'm a real pain in
the neck!" He raised his arm to his eyes as
if holding up a cape, then ran down the
hallway.

"That was weird," said Avery, behind
them.

Julian laughed. "It's just the catch
phrase from *Fangs for Nothing*," he
explained.

"Thanks for what?" Avery looked
puzzled.

"*Fangs for Nothing*," Lucy repeated.
"You know, the vampire show the whole
school is addicted to? A new episode drops
tomorrow night, and everyone is totally
excited about it." She grinned at Julian.
They both loved anything to do with

horror and watched the show together each week. They even wore vampire fangs left over from Lucy's birthday loot bags. Her mom had accidentally added an extra zero to their online order. Instead of twenty, they ended up with two hundred nonreturnable pairs of teeth!

Julian and Lucy lived in the same apartment building, which made hanging out really easy. Even though they were different, they were best friends. Sure, Lucy loved sports, and Julian was allergic to them. Julian was an artist, and Lucy couldn't draw a straight line. And Lucy spent her entire allowance each week, while Julian was a saver. But they saw eye to eye on everything else. Including cooking club—*bo-ring!*

Avery shrugged. "It's not on my radar," she said. "But maybe I'll give it a gander tonight. See you later!"

Lucy and Julian looked at each other, trying not to laugh. Avery, the new girl in school, talked like a grown-up sometimes. But she was kind and generous and was starting to grow on them.

They paused for a minute in front of the door to the school kitchen before Julian took a deep breath and pushed it open. The eight other members of the club spun around and stared at them. Even though Julian and Lucy were a little bit late, Ms. Clark was nowhere to be seen.

CHAPTER TWO

A third-grader named Caitlynne spoke up as Julian and Lucy grabbed seats. "Do you think cooking club is canceled?" she asked hopefully.

Just then the kitchen door swung open. A tall, dark-haired man walked to the front of the room and faced the students, a big smile on his face.

Julian turned to Lucy. "That's Mr. Lopez," Julian whispered to Lucy. "He's the new fifth-grade teacher."

"I'm Mr. Lopez, the new fifth-grade

teacher," the man said. "I'm going to be your club's advisor now. I love to cook, and I'm excited to share some of my favorite recipes with you."

Lucy elbowed Julian in the ribs. "He loves to cook? Sounds like Mr. Lopez is the anti-Ms. Clark," she said.

"Mr. Lopez is the coolest," he told her. "He has a special handshake for every kid in his class, and they line up to do it every morning."

But Mr. Lopez's next words sealed the deal. "I thought we'd make churros today. With strawberry dipping sauce." He clapped his hands together. "So, are you ready to start cooking?"

The class cheered. Finally, they were cooking something fun!

"We'll need water, flour, sugar, cinnamon, butter, salt, and eggs for the churro dough, and vegetable oil for frying them," Mr. Lopez explained. He turned and wrote the recipes for churro dough, cinnamon sugar— to roll the fried churros in—and strawberry sauce on the whiteboard.

As the students began gathering the ingredients, Mr. Lopez went through the cupboards. He placed spoons, bowls, saucepans, pastry bags, measuring cups, and a large frying pan on the counter.

While he heated up vegetable oil in the frying pan, he told everyone to pair up and start making the dough.

"By ourselves?" Theo asked in disbelief.

Mr. Lopez gave him a funny look. "Of course!" he said. "This is cooking club, isn't it? Just let me know if you have any questions."

The students exchanged excited glances and measured the water, sugar, salt, and butter and put it in their saucepans. Mr. Lopez *was* the anti-Ms. Clark! Then they took turns heating the ingredients on the stove. Julian and Lucy were third in line. After their mixture came to a boil, they turned down the heat and dumped in the flour. They stirred it until it began to form a ball, then removed the saucepan from the heat and added the eggs. The mixture got very thick.

"Great job, kids," said Mr. Lopez when everyone was done. "After the dough cools a bit, please put it into the pastry bags. Then line up so we can start frying the churros."

Lucy and Julian struggled to get their pastry bag filled, so they ended up last. Julian noticed that Lucy was frowning. She always liked to be first. But then she grinned. "Hey, Mr. Lopez!" she called out. "Could Julian and I make the strawberry

sauce while we're waiting for our turn?"

"Excellent idea!" he said. "Strawberries are in the fridge in the crisper drawer."

As Theo and Olivia squeezed lines of dough into the hot oil, the room began to fill with the delicious smell of fried churros. Lucy and Julian rinsed and chopped the strawberries, then put them into a saucepan with sugar, vanilla, and lemon juice. Soon the sauce was bubbling and ready to be blended.

Julian's mouth watered. He wanted a churro in his belly. Like right now.

He grabbed an oven mitt and carried the saucepan full of warm strawberry sauce over to the blender. After pouring it in, he plopped the lid on top. His finger hovered over the "blend" button.

Mr. Lopez turned around. "Hey Julian, make sure that lid is—"

CHAPTER THREE

"What?" said Julian, as he pressed the button.

BLAM! The lid flew off the top of the blender. Julian and Lucy watched in horror as bright red sauce shot out, splattering the walls, floors, counters, and to their complete shock, the principal. It looked like a scene straight out of *Fangs for Nothing.*

Yes, the principal. Ms. McDonnell had stepped inside the room at exactly the wrong moment.

". . . on tight," Mr. Lopez finished. He wiped some sauce off his cheek and tasted it. He smiled. "Delicious!" He turned to the principal. "Why, hello there, Ms. McDonnell. My sincerest apologies. Hoping you aren't allergic to strawberries?" He reached into his pocket and handed her a clean handkerchief.

"Thank you," she said, taking off her splattered glasses and wiping them. "Not a problem. I was just stopping by to check out the new banner. Coach Chang hung it up in here so I could take a look before the upcoming pep rally." She put her glasses back on, then looked around the room. Suddenly her face fell.

"Oh no," she said.

Julian spun around slowly. Yikes.
The brand-new banner was dripping
with pureed strawberries. He gulped. A
smear of sauce had changed the *R* to a
B. The banner now read SPRINGFIELD
SCHOOL STABS.

Ms. McDonnell blinked and took a deep breath. "I know our sports teams are out for blood, but this is ridiculous!" she finally said.

Mr. Lopez bit his lip. Grabbing a sponge and a stepladder he climbed up and started to wipe the banner. He scrubbed and scrubbed. But it was no use. It was ruined. Lucy reached over and gave Julian's hand a quick squeeze, for support. But Julian couldn't even look at her.

"It's okay," said Ms. McDonnell. "Accidents happen." She sighed. "We won't be able to replace the banner this year. It cost a hundred dollars, and there's just no more money in the budget."

"What's a budget?" Lucy whispered.

Julian shrugged. He had no idea. All he

knew was that he felt awful. Just awful.

After the principal left, Mr. Lopez picked up the platter of churros and walked around the room, offering them to the students.

When Mr. Lopez got to him and Lucy, Julian blurted out, "I'm sorry I ruined the banner."

"It wasn't your fault," Mr. Lopez assured him. "How were you supposed to know that you need to bang down the top of that old blender lid?" He smiled at them both. "Churro?" he asked.

Lucy took one of the treats, but Julian shook his head. He had lost his appetite.

CHAPTER FOUR

Julian was having a bad morning. He couldn't figure out the math problem his teacher had written on the whiteboard. In fact, he had just torn a hole in his notebook page from erasing so much.

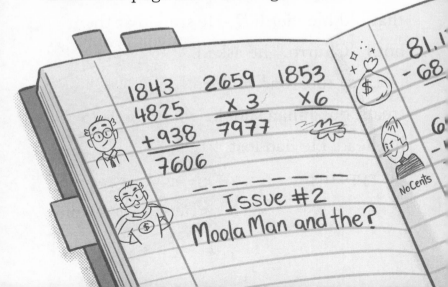

1843
4825
+938
7606

2659
x 3
7977

1853
x6

81,1
- 68

$

6
-

NoCents

Issue #2
Moola Man and the?

All he could think about was the disaster the day before and the ruined banner.

And now he had something new to worry about. On the way to school that morning, he and Lucy had run into a few of their cooking club friends. Maddy had said something that made his stomach sink. "What if Principal McDonnell fires Mr. Lopez and Ms. Clark becomes our adviser again?"

Everyone had been quiet for the rest of the walk to school. Remembering Maddy's words, Julian sighed and sank lower in his seat.

The next thing he knew, a folded-up piece of paper hit him in the head. He looked up, annoyed, before glancing at it. His name was written on the paper in very familiar handwriting. Curious, he opened it.

I have an idea how we can fix this. Let's meet the rest of the club in the yard after school today to talk about it.

☺ Okay?

He turned around. Lucy was staring at him, waiting for an answer. He nodded, and she gave him a thumbs-up.

He sat up straighter in his seat, feeling a bit more hopeful. If the cooking club put their heads together, maybe they'd be able to figure out how to fix this problem.

Maybe.

$ $ $

"I think it's pretty simple," said Lucy after school that day. The cooking club had gathered by the jungle gym. "We need to

24

raise money and replace the banner so Mr. Lopez can stay on as our adviser for sure."

"All right!" said Theo excitedly. Then he frowned. "But . . . um . . . how?"

They stared at each other blankly.

"What about a coin drive?" said Jackson. "You know when people bring in their spare change. They did one at my sister's high school."

Theo shook his head. "Coins are heavy," he said. "It's fine for high schoolers, but no way the littler kids would be able to carry much. We wouldn't raise a lot of money."

Julian's shoulders sagged.

"We need something fun that the whole school can do. Something we can charge for," said Lucy. "Something like . . . a carnival?"

"Ooooh!" said Ryan. "We could have rides and games and prizes and—"

"Too complicated," said Caitlynne, cutting him off. "There's not enough time with the pep rally in two weeks."

"I know!" Julian suddenly heard himself saying. Everyone turned to stare at him. "We're in a cooking club, right? How about a bake sale?"

Lucy punched Julian in the arm. "You're a genius!" she said. "We can bake next week in cooking club and sell everything at lunchtime the next day!"

"If we each chip in four dollars, we would have forty dollars to spend on the bake sale," said Caitlynne. "We'd get our money back after."

Everyone started talking at once. What

27

treats should they make? How many? How much would they sell them for?

Julian had another idea. "My mom can help us!" he shouted above the chatter. The other kids stopped talking and turned toward him. "She's a caterer. Her job is to make all sorts of food for parties and work events. She's good at coming up with menus and knows lots of recipes. And she's home right now. Want to come over?"

"Will she serve snacks?" Theo wanted to know.

Julian nodded. "Definitely."

Ella Jean had to go to the dentist, but the others could all come. Julian and Lucy led the way to their apartment building. Caitlynne fell into step beside them. "Are you sure your mom isn't going to freak out when we get there?" she asked. "If I just showed up with eight hungry friends my moms would both flip!"

Lucy laughed. "Oh no, Julian's mom always says as long as she's at home, he can invite as many friends over as he wants," she explained. "And she *always* has good snacks!"

That was true, but Julian couldn't help feeling a little bit nervous. Were eight friends about six friends too many?

CHAPTER FIVE

"Welcome!" Julian's mom said when she opened the front door. She smiled broadly. "Good timing! I'm testing out a new recipe, and I just took a batch of mac and cheese bites out of the oven."

Theo and Ryan high-fived.

Whew. Julian breathed a sigh of relief. If his mom was surprised to see so many kids on her doorstep, she didn't show it. She held the door open as they filed in and left their shoes, jackets, and backpacks in a big mountain by the entrance.

"Lucky for you the twins are at a playdate," she said to Julian as he walked inside.

Julian nodded. He loved his sisters Abby and Gabby, but he was pretty sure they would have made everyone play dress-up with them or something equally embarrassing. They were only four years old, after all.

The cooking club kids gathered around the kitchen counter. His mom poured glasses of lemonade as Julian reminded her of the cooking club disaster. She looked at her son sympathetically. "I should have warned you about blenders. You should have seen me at my very first catering job. Pea soup, everywhere! It took me hours to clean it up."

Then Lucy told Julian's mom about their money-raising idea. After placing the platter of mac and cheese bites on the counter, she wiped her hands on her apron. "So, what are you thinking of making for this bake sale?" she asked.

Even though their mouths were full, everyone started excitedly shouting out ideas. Make-your-own ice-cream cookie sandwiches! Cream puffs! Macarons *and*

macaroons! Brownies and blondies and cupcakes and whoopie pies! A chocolate fountain!

Lucy reached for another mac and cheese bite. "Don't forget doughnuts," she said. Julian grinned. They were Lucy's favorite treats of all time. She even had a doughnut cake at her last birthday party.

"Whoa," said Julian's mom. "That's a lot of treats!"

"Well, we need to make a lot of money," said Ryan. "So we need to sell a lot of things."

"You must have a really big budget to be able to make so many different things to sell," Julian's mom said.

There was that word again. The cooking club got quiet.

"What's a budget?" Caitlynne finally asked.

"It's an estimate of your income and expenses," Julian's mom explained. "It's what you need to figure out before you start any project."

The kids just stared at her.

"Expenses are what you spend. Income is how much money you make. Your income needs to be bigger than your expenses to make a profit," she told them. "The profit is the money that you will use to buy the new banner."

"Um . . . okay?" said Cora.

Julian gulped. This bake sale stuff was way more complicated than he had imagined.

CHAPTER SIX

Julian's mom closed her eyes for a moment, then opened them and smiled. She held up a mac and cheese bite.

"Before I can add these to my catering menu, I have to figure out how much they cost me to make—that's my expense. I also have to figure out how much I can charge for them—that's my income. Then I subtract the expense from the income. That's my profit."

"I think I get it," said Lucy. But she didn't sound so sure.

"Okay," Julian's mom said. "Let's add it up. What are my ingredients?"

"Macaroni!"

"Cheese!"

"Um . . . breadcrumbs?"

Julian's mom nodded. "Plus milk, flour, spices, eggs, and butter. Let's say I want to make one hundred bites and the ingredients will cost me . . ." She thought for a moment. "Around twenty-five dollars."

The kids all nodded.

A timer went off. Julian's mom slipped on a pair of oven mitts. She opened the oven and took out another tray of mac and cheese bites. Theo reached for one.

"Just a minute! They need to cool first."

Julian's mom put down the tray. "So back to our budget. If I charge two dollars a bite and I sell them all—"

"You'll make two hundred dollars!" said Olivia.

"Not so fast," said Julian's mom. "Remember my expenses? I bought all the ingredients. I have to subtract that cost to find out how much I really made. Income

$ 200 - $ 25 = $ 175

income - expenses = profit

minus expenses equals profit. So, two hundred minus twenty-five is one hundred and seventy-five. And one hundred and seventy-five dollars—"

"—is your profit," said Lucy. "Now I get it!" Other kids were nodding, too. Julian smiled at his mom proudly.

She grabbed a spatula and moved the appetizers onto a serving plate. Theo was the first to grab one. Julian's mom ate a bite, too.

"Not bad if I do say so myself," she said. "Now let's get down to business and figure out what you can make for your bake sale. How much money do you have to spend on your ingredients?"

"Four dollars times the ten of us," said Caitlynne. "That equals forty dollars."

Julian's mom nodded. "So, with the size of your school, figure you'll want to make about two hundred treats." She paused. "With forty dollars to spend, you only have enough money to buy ingredients for one type of treat."

"One treat!" Ryan groaned. "That's all?"

"No chocolate fountain?" Theo asked. "Bummer."

Julian's mom nodded. "It is a bummer. Now, the next thing to think about is market capture. That means knowing what your customers want. Of all the treats you mentioned, which one do you think will appeal the most to the students at your school?"

"Doughnuts!" said Lucy without hesitation. "They serve them in the cafeteria once in a while and everyone goes wild."

"Works for me," said Jackson.

Caitlynne nodded. "Yum."

Olivia shook her head. "Don't you need special pans to make doughnuts? We can't afford that expense on our budget."

"That's exactly right," said Julian's mom. "But I have a surprise for you!" She ducked behind the kitchen counter. There was the sound of crashing pots and pans. "You'll never guess what I just bought for the birthday party I catered last week!"

"Doughnut pans?" asked Lucy hopefully.

Julian's mom popped up. "Doughnut pans!" she said. She held one in each hand. "And I'm happy to lend them to you."

Lucy cheered. The rest of the kids joined in.

"Now we have to figure out how much to charge for each doughnut," said Julian's mom. "Remember that your price needs to be high enough to make a profit but low enough that kids will buy a lot of them.

41

We know we need to raise one hundred dollars plus—"

"Forty dollars for the ingredients," finished Maddy.

Julian's mom nodded. "Very good."

Jackson spoke up. "So if we need to make at least one hundred forty dollars, we can charge one dollar for each doughnut and still have extra money."

"If you can make a profit by charging a dollar for a doughnut does that mean you should charge two dollars a doughnut and make even more money?" Julian's mom asked.

Silence.

Finally, Lucy spoke up. "I don't think so. We're selling to kids, and most of them don't have a lot of money. We'll probably sell more doughnuts if we keep the price down."

"What do the rest of you think about that?" asked Julian's mom. "Do you agree that we should charge a dollar a doughnut?"

Everyone thought for a minute, then one by one, they nodded.

"And that is called knowing your audience," said Julian's mom. She smiled at the friends proudly. "My work here is done!"

CHAPTER SEVEN

"I can't believe the bake sale is tomorrow," Lucy said as she and Julian walked to school.

"I know!" said Julian. A little shiver ran down his spine. He wasn't sure if it was excitement or nerves. Probably both.

It had been a very busy week. On Tuesday afternoon, Mr. Lopez took the club members shopping for the ingredients. In the checkout line, Julian told everyone what he had learned from his mom at dinner the night before.

"Advertising is a very important part of a business. That means informing your customers about your product."

On Wednesday, they made posters to hang all around the school. Luckily the groceries had only cost thirty-three dollars. So even with the five dollars they spent on paper, they were still under budget. It also helped that the art teacher loaned them some markers.

COOKING CLUB BAKE SALE FUNDRAISER
This Friday at lunchtime
Bring your appetite!
And your $!

Now it was Thursday. Cooking club. When the end-of-the-school-day bell rang, Julian and Lucy jumped out of their seats and practically raced to the kitchen. It was time to make the doughnuts.

Mr. Lopez stood in the front of the room, beaming. "I still can't believe you're doing a fundraiser to replace the banner. You guys rock!" He put on an apron that said BAKE THE WORLD A BETTER PLACE. "This is going to be so much fun."

"If you say so," said Theo. He was still upset there wasn't going to be a chocolate fountain.

Mr. Lopez laughed. "I just did."

Julian placed the doughnut pans on the kitchen counter next to a huge bag of sugar. There was an even bigger bag of flour and several cartons of eggs. Baking powder and salt. Milk, butter, and vanilla extract. Bowls, spoons, and piping bags.

Julian and Lucy measured the dry ingredients. Theo dumped them into the giant bowl and Caitlynne whisked them. Olivia poured the milk. Maddy melted the butter. Ryan and Jackson cracked the eggs, and Ella Jean and Cora stirred it all together. Then they poured the dough into the bags and piped it into the pans.

"Mom says only three-quarters of the way up," Julian warned. "Otherwise we'll end up with doughnuts without holes!"

When the doughnut pans were in the oven, Theo asked to be excused.

"When you gotta go, you gotta go," said Ryan.

"Shall we make the glaze?" asked Mr. Lopez. As the doughnuts baked, and the room began to fill with the cozy smell of vanilla, they mixed the ingredients.

Just then the door burst open. Theo stood in the entranceway, looking pale as a ghost.

"This is terrible!" he said.

Caitlynne sighed. "Theo, we're sorry there's no chocolate fountain, but the doughnuts are going to be a big hit tomorrow. Get over it."

Theo shook his head. "That's not it," he said. "I just ran into the lunch lady. She asked me if I was excited for tomorrow."

"What's tomorrow?" Olivia asked.

"Doughnut Day in the cafeteria!" Theo told them.

CHAPTER EIGHT

"What are we going to do?" Jackson cried.

"Can we ask the lunch lady not to make them?" Ella Jean asked.

Theo shook his head. "Already made," he said.

"Looks like we've got some competition, kids," said Mr. Lopez. "But I'm sure our doughnuts will still be a hit with the students."

"Why would they buy our doughnuts when they can have free ones?" said Cora.

Julian gave Lucy a worried look. Cora had a good point.

The students were quiet as the doughnuts came out of the oven. After they cooled, the kids dipped them into the glaze and placed them on racks to dry.

When they were done, they stared down at their creation.

"These doughnuts look . . . ," Olivia started to say.

"Boring," Theo finished.

Julian felt his heart sink. The doughnuts *did* look boring.

"Maybe some color?" Lucy suggested. She found a container of rainbow sprinkles in the cupboard and shook it on top of one of the doughnuts.

Theo shook his head. "Our doughnuts have to be special," he said. "These are not special."

"Do you have any ideas? Or are you just going to complain?" snapped Olivia.

"I'm just going to complain," said Theo. He shrugged. "Hey! Maybe there's still time to do the chocolate fountain?"

When everyone groaned, he lifted his arm to his face as if he was raising the edge of a cape. "Sorry," he said. "I'm a real pain in the neck!"

Olivia rolled her eyes, but Julian gasped. "That's it!" he cried.

He ran over to the cupboard and found tubes of pre-made frosting left over from the Ms. Clark days. He grabbed three—red, black, and white.

"I think this might just work," he said as he began decorating one of the doughnuts.

Ella Jean frowned. "I um, don't get it," she said. "What is it supposed to be?"

"Lucy, can I have your backpack?" he asked.

Lucy gave him a puzzled look, but

handed it to him. Julian rummaged in the front pocket until he found what he was looking for. He placed it inside the doughnut hole and stepped back.

"Ohhhhhh!" said the kids when they realized what he had done.

"That's awesome," Theo cried. "Julian, you are a genius!"

$ $ $

"Dracula Doughnuts!" cried Avery. "Oh my goodness, how clever. I'll wear these teeth when I watch *Fangs for Nothing* tonight!"

Kids crowded around the table, jockeying for position. "These are the coolest!" a third-grader said.

The cooking club was handing out

doughnuts and collecting dollars as fast as they could. After a while, Julian looked down. Not a single doughnut was left.

"I just want to say . . . fangs for your support!" said Mr. Lopez. He had shown up to the bake sale wearing a long black cape and a set of vampire teeth. "You all pitched in and worked together. You really did your research and learned how to run a business. We made a revenue of two hundred dollars and a profit of one hundred and sixty-two dollars!"

Julian sighed with relief. They had reached their goal. They made enough profit to replace the banner and then some. Everything was going to be okay.

"After we give Principal McDonnell the one hundred dollars to buy the new banner, we have sixty-two dollars left for our club," said Mr. Lopez. "What do you think we should do with the money?"

"Buy some doughnut pans!" said Lucy.

At the same time Julian said, "Save it for a rainy day!"

Mr. Lopez laughed. "Why not both?"

MOOLA MAN'S MONEY MATTERS
The Lemon Squeeze by Julian J.

JUST IN CASE YOU DIDN'T READ ISSUE #1, OR YOU HAVE A BAD MEMORY, MR. MIKE MORRIS WAS AN ORDINARY MATH TEACHER UNTIL HE WAS STRUCK BY LIGHTNING WHILE USING AN ATM.

NOW, WHENEVER A CITIZEN IN MEGALOPOLIS IS IN FINANCIAL DISTRESS, HIS WALLET STARTS TO TINGLE AND HE TRANSFORMS INTO MOOLA MAN!

DOLLARS and SENSE: BUDGETING

Thanks to Julian's kitchen disaster, the Cooking Club had to make some money—and fast. They soon figured out that they needed a budget. Otherwise, they might have spent all their money and not made a profit!

Can you make and stick to a budget? Here's how:

1) First figure out what your goal is. Are you hoping to buy something big?
2) How much time do you have? Is there a deadline?
3) How much income will you get during this time? List your allowance and money you earn from chores or doing odd jobs. Is your birthday or a holiday coming up when people might give you money? Include those, too!
4) List your expenses during that time period. Do you go out with friends after school? Do you need poster board and markers for a school project?
5) Is your income larger than your expenses? It should be.
6) Make a spending plan and stick to it.

And that's a budget!

GOAL: SKATEBOARD ($100)	TIME TO GOAL: 6 MONTHS
INCOME	MONTHLY EXPENSES
ALLOWANCE ($7 A WEEK) WALK NEIGHBOR'S DOG ($20 A MONTH) BIRTHDAY MONEY ($55)	AFTER SCHOOL SNACKS ($15) GAMING COSTS ($5) ACTIVITIES WITH FRIENDS ($20)
TOTAL FOR 6 MONTHS: $343	TOTAL FOR 6 MONTHS: $240
$343 (INCOME) − $240 (EXPENSES) = $103 YOU DID IT!	

Want to get the skateboard even more quickly? Try to cut back on expenses until you reach that goal. Or see if you can pick up extra work. Maybe Fido needs more walks!

Don't miss book #3
in the Dollars to Doughnuts series!

Julian has saved his pennies—and quarters and
dollars—for ages. He keeps them in a safe place, at
the top of the closet, behind his winter blanket in
his trusty piggy bank, Wilbur. But now his mom, his
dad, even his best friend Lucy, who barely saves any
money at all, says Wilbur isn't safe *enough*. They
want him to move his money to a bank! A piggy bank
is a perfectly safe place to stash cash—isn't it?

For more, visit kanepress.com